Cats versus Cat Burglars

by Craig Joseph Pisani

illustrated by Becca Lippe

Tank

Mika

MAC

little

It was a stressful night at the DiPaolo house. Lauren and Joe received a call from the local cat shelter explaining that a lack of funding would force them to close their doors forever. The importance of the shelter, not only personally but to the entire community, made them realize they needed to help, but how? They discussed it all day but soon dozed on the couch, surrounded by their equally exhausted special needs cats that were busy all day napping and eating each other's food.

There's LITTLE, the big baby who struggles to walk because of a rare brain condition called Cerebellar Hypoplasia which impacts his motor skills, MIKA, the blind beauty, MAC, the nasally-noised cleft palate cutie with half a nostril which makes him sound like a gremlin, LEELA, the one eyed toughie, and resting ever so peacefully like a king in the upstairs bedroom, the bow-legged runt of the litter...

Achoo!

Lauren's lids slowly sunk until Leela let out the faintest of sneezes. "Joe, wake up!" Lauren said while tugging on his shirt. "Is it time to go to work?" Joe replied.

"Worse. Leela's sick. We have to take her to the vet!" cried the worried mom. "Are you sure?" said the sleepy cat dad.

"Huh? I'm not sick!" screamed the feisty feline. But to human ears all that could be heard was a loud, drawn-out MEOOOOOOOOW.

"See, that's a yes," said Lauren; "Get the carrying crate."

"What are ya kidding me? It was one measly sneeze," explained Leela.

"Joe, hurry, it's worse than I thought.

"Bye, Leela.
Say 'Hi' to Doctor
Ruderman for me,"
said Little.

"None of you better
sit in my chair while I'm gone,"
stated Leela.

"That wouldn't be
this one by any chance,
would it? I am blind
you know," teased Mika.

"Yes it is!" said Leela.

"Sorry Leela, I can't hear
you. I think I may be going deaf
as well," Mika said sarcastically.
She snuggled deeper into the
chair as Lauren escorted Leela
away for her date
with the doctor.

An hour went by before
DING DONG! DING DONG!

The late night doorbell chimes woke the surprised cats from their sound slumber. Mac dopily trotted towards the front door to greet his guests but Mika and Little sensed that something was not quite right at this hour.

BANG! SPLIT! CRACK!

The broken door gingerly creaked open. Mika yanked Mac out of the way before being seen.

The most wanted thieves in town, Nine Lives Nancy and her husband Dirty Boot Bobby—whose filthy, cruddy soles leaves footprints with each step—entered the home ready to ransack the house.

"Everyone outside, right away!" said the quick-thinking Mika.

"Who were those people?" Little asked. "Cat burglars," answered Mika. "They take people's cats?!?" assumed Little. "No, don't be ridiculous. They are bad people who steal things from people's homes. I heard about them on the news," said Mika, "There's no mistaking this disgusting crud I stepped in."
"Oh no! She's right! Look at the tree! Let's get far away from here," said Little.
"Wait! We forgot about Tank! We have to go back in and bring him with us," said Mika.

WANTED

Dirty Boot Bobby   Nine Lives Nancy

REWARD

"But I'm too small," whined Little. "Little, I don't know if you know this, but you're not that little."

"We can't do it. We aren't like regular cats."
"That's not true."
"Well it is."

"Let me scout out the situation first," said Mika.

"That's not working. Put your ear against the glass!

"They seem like nice people. Maybe we shouldn't take too much stuff," said Nancy before spotting a semi-sleeping Tank yawning on the bed. "Oh... my... goodness, forget that...

...look what I found!!"
Tank awoke from nap time, shocked that this wild-haired wacko picked him up. He bit, clawed, and hissed but she held him even tighter.

"Look Bobby, he likes me."

What!?

Mika returned. "See, just like a regular cat would do," said Mika.

"You were lucky the owl was there to help," said Little.

"We have to act fast, she's already got him," said Mika.

"I think I'm going to stay right here where it's safe," Little said defiantly.

"But it's the middle of winter, you might catch a cold."

"That's what my fur is for."

"But the sky is cloudy, it may rain."

"Then I'll take shelter under that tree."

Mac snorts out some panicking gremlin noises.

Mika whispered,
"Little, don't look now but
Mac says there is a hawk in
that tree and he looks
very hungry."

"Where?" questioned Little as he
frantically spun around to see.

"We must go insi-"

Little did not wait for Mika
to finish talking. He already
scampered back into the house.

"First, we'll need to get to the second floor," said Mika.

"But I can't climb stairs," Little said shamefully.

"Little, that is the first thing you said all day that made any sense. We will help you. That's what family is for."

"Now we must sneak into the bedroom unnoticed," said Mika.

Mac generated some gremlin noises and pointed down the hall.

"Good thinking MAC-aroni! We'll hide behind that potted plant until the burglar passes."

The flushing sound did the trick as Nancy placed Tank down on the bed then entered the bathroom to investigate.

Mac hid and laughed while Nancy jiggled the handle of the toilet bowl.

"This toilet mustn't be working properly. It's making weird noises."

Snort

WOOOOOSH!!!!

"Tank! It's us!" announced Little. Tank peered over the ledge of the mattress and smiled at his siblings. "Jump! We will take you to safety," said Mika.

Tank took a few steps backwards for a running start. He leaped off the bed but Nancy caught him in midair.

"Oh no you don't! You're coming with me," said the cat burglar. Little and Mika hid while Nancy imprisoned Tank in his carrying crate and brought him downstairs.

"I told you they take people's cats," Little bragged. "Yes, but now is not the time for boasting. We need a new plan or Tank will be gone forever." Mac produced his famous gremlin noises. "Mac, you're a genius! When in trouble dial 911! But the only phone is downstairs on the kitchen table," Mika pointed out. "I have an idea," said Little.

"Stop picking up all the cat toys and steal something of value!" said Bobby. "No! This tiny one needs all his toys to play with at our home. Got it?" Nancy said convincingly. "Yes dear. It is time for us to go. Grab the crate and let's get out of here."

"Quick! Aim the sled right at them, Little. We'll knock them down like bowling pins!" ordered Mika.

Little kicked strongly, launching them down the steps.

The kitten crew jumped off in a nick of time as the sled crashed into the burglars, sending Nancy flying out the front door feet first. Mac closed the door behind her. "More cats? Scram! Get out of here," Bobby said angrily. "Split up. I'll make a run for the phone," said Mika.

Bobby chased the cats throughout the house:

He trapped Little in the flameless fireplace.

Mac wandered into an open closet filled with assorted holiday decorations. Bobby slid the door shut.

Mika sprinted towards the kitchen table. She nearly made it but Bobby jumped in front of her path with a collar and leash in hand. He corralled the cutie and double-knot tied her to a doorknob.

Little contemplated the
great escape.

Mac bounced a cat toy ball
off the wall.

Mika reached for the phone
but the leash wasn't long enough.

Tank's crate broke during the fall. He stuck his paw through the gate and easily pried it open.

Like a miniature ninja, he snuck past Bobby who was preoccupied regathering his stolen items.

Mika felt defeated.
Her face buried in her paws.
Suddenly, Tank entered the room,
rejuvenating her spirits!

"Tank, you're okay! I was so
worried about you," she said.

"Thank you. Now let's cut you free
and save the others," suggested Tank.

"I can't. My claws were just trimmed."

"Mine weren't!" Tank said slyly as he sliced
the leash in half with his sharp claw.

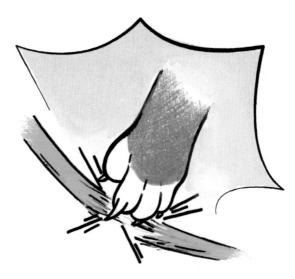

Mika leaped onto the kitchen table.
She wanted to dial the number but suddenly
stopped. "What's wrong, Mika?"
Tank called out from the floor.

"I can't see the numbers to dial for help,"
said Mika.

"I can but I am too tiny to jump on
the table," replied Tank.

"Then we will use teamwork. Here, hold onto
the leash and I will pull you up."

Little gave maximum effort attempting to escape the fireplace.

"Little? I don't even recognize you anymore," said Tank.

"Must be a bad hair day," teased Mika.

"Mika, your jokes are as bad as your eyesight. Now get me outta here!"

Mac bounced the ball off the wall even harder, causing the vibrations to knock a scary mask off the shelf and onto his head. He shook and shook but it would not come off.

The door to the closet slid open...

It's Mika, Tank and Little to the rescue!

Mac bolted out wildly past his siblings desperate to dislodge the mask.

Mac's gremlin noises echoed throughout the house. The noise grew louder, grabbing Bobby's attention as it drew nearer to him. Mac headed straight for Bobby, scaring the crud off his dirty, filthy boots.

"What kind of animal is that?!?"

"Send him my way Mac!" yelled Little from the living room.

Bobby zoomed past Little who fiercely shook himself clean, creating a soot storm.

"Look Mika, just like a regular cat."

"Yes! I'm so proud of you, Little."

"I can't see," said Bobby. "I'm blind!"

"Welcome to my world," said Mika as she kicked litter out of the box and all over the floor, creating a slippery mess.

Bobby slid face first into Leela's favorite chair, completely destroying it. The gremlin noises approached yet again.

Bobby staggered to his feet. With great haste,
he exited the house blowing past Nancy.

"More cats!" screamed Nancy as she scooped them up and squeezed tightly. "Now you will all come home with me and cuddle, and love, and play, and take pictures, and post videos," said a love struck Nancy who suddenly stopped speaking upon seeing...

In Memory of Tiny Tank 7/23/16-8/21/17

Although fictional in story, the
truth is that animal shelters do in fact need
our help in continuing to offer vital services to the
community such as overpopulation control, low cost
veterinary services, and shelter to stray or abandoned
animals with the intent of finding them
a permanent home.

Actions speak louder than words.
We will be donating a portion of the proceeds
from the sale of this book to a variety of animal
shelters; especially ones which are special
needs cat friendly of course.

Dedicated to our Mom and Dad
and the cats that started it all:
Taffy, Tiger, Shadow, and Sushi.

Special thanks to Andrew Grandner,
Mark A. Langston, Dr. Irwin Ruderman,
Dr. Liz Houston, and Matthew Simon.

Made in the USA
Middletown, DE
20 February 2019